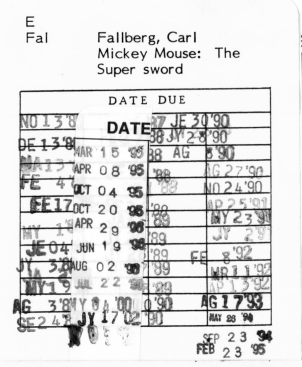
W9-AJT-171

WALT DISNEY
MICKEY MOUSE
THE SUPER SWORD

by CARL FALLBERG
illustrated by PAUL MURRY

A GOLDEN BOOK · NEW YORK
Western Publishing Company, Inc., Racine, Wisconsin 53404

Copyright ©1967 by Walt Disney Productions. All rights reserved. Printed in the U.S.A. by Western Publishing Company, Inc. No part of this book may be reproduced or copied in any form without written permission from the copyright owner. GOLDEN®, A GOLDEN BOOK®, and GOLDEN & DESIGN® are trademarks of Western Publishing Company, Inc. Library of Congress Catalog Card Number: 84-073245. ISBN 0-307-11934-3/ISBN 0-307-61934-6 (lib. bdg.) A B C D E F G H I J

Mickey and Goofy, transported back through time in a fantastic time machine, landed in medieval England. Deciding to stay awhile, they set up a business and soon became experts at making horseshoes and swords.

Then one day Mickey fashioned a sword that he knew was special. It radiated power—super power!

"It is super sharp and rugged," said Mickey proudly. "I'm going to give this sword to our king."

An instant later they heard shouts of HELP! and EEK! coming from outside. Mickey and Goofy ran to their door to see what was happening.

The townspeople were in a panic. Approaching shore was a ship full of fierce Viking warriors. Even worse, it was the ship of the most dreaded Viking of all...

It's Veric the Red!

"Come on, Goofy," called Mickey, "we'd better flee, too."

But just then a damsel's shriek pierced the air.

EEEEEEEEEEEK!

Mickey turned and ran to offer aid. He then saw that Veric the Red had captured the king's daughter, lovely Princess Minnie.

"Unhand her, you big red-bearded lout!" demanded Mickey, waving his sword.

Veric the Red dropped Minnie and laughed as he moved toward Mickey.
"Ho-ho! Do you have any last words?"

Mickey thought he had Veric the Red at his mercy, but a Viking raider tossed a barrel over Mickey, knocking the super sword from his hand.

"I must have that sword," said Veric. "It cut mine right in two!"

"With this sword, I can raid any town, any country," boasted Veric. "Now, Vikings, load our plunder aboard. It is time to sail."

Princess Minnie was put on board the Viking ship, for Veric the Red knew that he could get a fine ransom from her father, the king.

Mickey and Goofy were put to work as oarsmen. "Thuh blisters on my hands are gettin' blisters," sighed Goofy.

Goofy's sore hands slipped from the oar, and Goofy tumbled back into the oarsman behind him…

…and *that* oarsman bumped the oarsman behind him…and *that* oarsman bumped the oarsman behind him. On and on it went.

"Quick, Goofy," whispered Mickey, "this is our chance to escape." An instant later they both jumped overboard.

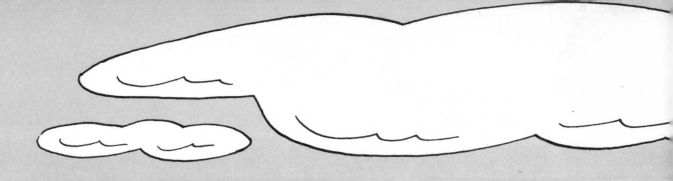

Reaching shore, Mickey glanced back at the Viking ship. "They're going into that sheltered inlet. That's where their camp must be."

Goofy was more concerned about something that had slipped into his hat.

FLOP!

FLOP!

"Well, gawrshzooks," said the surprised Goofy as he emptied his hat.
"I guess I've got our dinner."

Mickey sat down and sighed. "Now all we have to do is get the super sword and rescue Princess Minnie."

Early the next morning, Mickey and Goofy reached the Vikings' camp. "They're probably asleep," said Mickey, "but we'd better get some branches to conceal ourselves, just in case."

They tiptoed down to the camp, and then, without warning...

"Sorry, Mickey," sniffled Goofy, "but there must be somethin' in thuh air that's givin' me thuh sneezes."

Mickey quickly tied a handkerchief around Goofy's nose to prevent him from sneezing again. Then they moved on, quietly.

"We can escape in that little sailboat," said Mickey, "as soon as we find Princess Minnie and get the sword."

A moment later, Mickey slipped past a sleeping
guard and found Princess Minnie.

Mickey's heart skipped a beat as he led Princess
Minnie out of the hut, for the guard was waking...

Suddenly...

Goofy's nose started twitching. "I think I'm gonna sneeze," he said.

Mickey acted fast. He grabbed a bucket and pushed it over Goofy's head, hoping to stop—or muffle—the sneeze.

The explosion propelled the bucket like a shot...

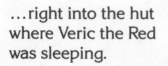

...right into the hut where Veric the Red was sleeping.

"Who hit me with a bucket?" bellowed Veric the Red.

Mickey ordered Goofy and Princess Minnie to run to the boat and cast off. "I'll stall them—and then meet you on the other side of the bay."

Mickey jumped in front of Veric the Red, and the chase was on.

"If I can make him mad enough," thought Mickey, "he might do something dumb and give me a chance to get the super sword."

Veric, unable to catch the fleet-footed Mickey, got madder and madder. But it was Mickey who then did a foolish thing by getting cornered in front of a stack of herring barrels.

But just then a well-aimed barrel landed on top of Veric, knocking the sword from his hand.

Mickey grabbed the super sword and ran toward the bay. He was surprised to see that Goofy and Princess Minnie had not sailed away.

What's wrong?

No wind!

SKRAAK!

PLUCK!

Acting fast, Mickey plucked a feather from a nearby chicken…

…and then he hopped aboard the sailboat and tickled Goofy's nose.

TICKLE! TICKLE!

Goofy's sneezes blew the sailboat out to sea, beyond arrow range of the pursuing Vikings.

"I've lost the sword *and* the ransom for the princess," grumbled Veric, "all because of that pip-squeak herring."

Meanwhile, the "pip-squeak herring" was being surprised with a thank-you kiss.

"You brave, wonderful rescuer," gushed Princess Minnie.

The Vikings, fearing Mickey and the super sword, stayed clear of the kingdom's shores. As a reward, the king signed an official document proclaiming Mickey and Goofy special court armorers!

So Mickey and Goofy stopped making horseshoes and made armor for the king and his officials—some of whom were as big as horses.

"This job could keep us here forever," said Goofy, chuckling.

"I like it," replied Mickey. And to himself he said, "I also like seeing Princess Minnie from time to time. She's cute!"